Dear Reader:

There's nothing like a good mystery with all the ingredients for a great time.

It's summer — a super time to solve a mystery. The setting is a big, old resort hotel on an island in New Hampshire, where a variety of people have come to enjoy their vacation. It seems, however, that one person is determined to destroy everyone's holiday fun.

This story involves three friends — Annie, Wallace, and Dave. You may recognize them from *Mystery of the Lobster Thieves* (also a Weekly Reader Book) where they helped find out who was robbing local fishermen's lobster traps. So these three young sleuths are at it again.

You'll never guess the ending! Isn't that the best kind of mystery? If it's too easy to figure out, it's not as much fun. Right up until the last chapter, you'll be wondering who is starting these island fires.

The author, Elaine Macmann Willoughby, has a knack for creating exciting and believable stories. She lives on an island in New England herself — wonder where she got the idea for the story?

We hope you have fun trying to solve this mystery!

Sincerely,

Stephen Fraser

Stephen Fraser
Senior Editor
Weekly Reader Book Club

Weekly Reader Book Club Presents

Mystery *of the* Island Fires

Elaine Macmann Willoughby

Illustrated by Janet Hamlin

Newfield Publications
Middletown, Connecticut

This book is an original presentation of Newfield Publications, Inc.
Newfield Publications offers book clubs for children
from preschool through high school. For further
information write to: **Newfield Publications, Inc.,**
4343 Equity Drive, Columbus, Ohio 43228.

Newfield Publications is a federally registered trademark of
Newfield Publications, Inc.
Weekly Reader is a federally registered trademark
of Weekly Reader Corporation.

Copyright © 1991 Elaine Macmann Willoughby
Cover art and text illustrations © 1991 Newfield Publications, Inc.

Illustrations by Janet Hamlin.
Editor: Stephen Fraser   Designer: David L. Brady

ISBN 0-8374-0118-6

Printed in the United States of America.

To Marcia Brown

1

The Island

I had never thought much about people having their house set on fire. At least not before our second summer at Blue Shutters. Blue Shutters is a little white cottage—with blue shutters, of course—that we rent for the summer. It's on an island, just off the coast of New Hampshire.

The cottage is on a small cove, with a rowboat anchored about ten feet from the house. You can fish and swim, and the nearby apple trees are great for climbing. Late in the summer the good apples are made into pies. The rotten ones we sometimes use for ammunition in our apple wars. Getting hit with a rotten apple doesn't hurt much, but it's very messy.

Besides all the apple trees there's a big oak tree. Wallace, my eleven-year-old brother, hung a swing from it. Good and bad things happened with that old oak tree. In the end I guess you'd say that the oak tree was the reason the mystery of the fires was solved. It might even have saved our lives. Imagine a tree saving your life!

We thought we'd left most of our vacation things in the cottage over the winter so that we wouldn't have to haul much stuff in our van when we went back at the beginning of the summer. But before we were through packing, we were as jammed as ever. And it was uncomfortably hot the day we moved out to the island.

Wallace grunted as he helped Dad lug a footlocker down the stairs of our apartment building. Mother looked at all the boxes and suitcases still to go and shook her head. "We're taking only the bare necessities, so I just don't understand how our things can make such a pile."

My three-year-old sister, Josie, had crawled into the front seat of the van. She didn't want to be left behind! This would have been OK except she was so hot that she kept wanting to take off all of her clothes. "Annie," my mother said as she squeezed another suitcase into the back seat, "please see that Josie stays dressed while we're packing the car."

I was stuck! And Josie was quite determined to make herself as cool as possible. I finally gave her some ice chips to suck while I read her a few stories.

Finally, after endless trips, everything had been lugged down from the apartment. The gerbil cage had been put temporarily on the front seat. Wallace and I were squeezed so tightly in the back seat that Josie had to sit in front with Mom and Dad. There certainly wasn't any room between us for the gerbil cage. And since neither one of us wanted to hold the cage on our lap for the two-hour drive, this created a problem—and we had a big fight. It began with Dad's saying, "I cannot drive this car while sitting on top of a gerbil cage. So one of you will have to hold the cage on your lap." He reached around and put the cage on Wallace's lap. But Wallace didn't want it, so he banged it down onto my lap. This jarred the cage's door latch and it flew open! The gerbils probably thought there was an earthquake, so they got all frightened and split out of the cage and under the front seat of the car. It's a bad scene when gerbils move out into the world on their own.

Dad quickly reached under the front seat and grabbed first one and then the other gerbil. After some rather stern words from him, things settled down. Wallace gave the gerbils some lettuce bits from the lunch basket and made the door latch tight. With the gerbils OK, from then on, we took half-hour turns holding the cage.

Wallace and I drew lots for the window seat and he lost, which was nice—for me. Our car quickly sped through the city traffic and in a short time we got on the thruway that led to New Hampshire. "Now I'm beginning to get excited," I said as I remembered the sand castles and fishing and all the fun we had had last summer in our little cottage.

"Cities are nice for winter," said Wallace, "but they're full of concrete and buildings and all of the things that hold heat. Come summer, I'm all for the bright blue sea!" As he reached into the picnic basket for an early start on lunch, he added, "You know, Annie, I can almost feel a mystery brewing already—and I'm quite positive I can smell a cool sea breeze!"

Mother groaned. "I certainly hope you're dead wrong about the first part of your statement."

Well, that's Wallace and his imagination. Mother says that Wallace can think of more things in five minutes that thrill or frighten him than most people can in a lifetime. Of course, last summer, along with our friend Dave Stone, we did get involved in the mystery of the lobster thieves. And before it was all over we had been kidnapped, which was pretty scary. *That* wasn't just Wallace's imagination!

Sometimes minutes can seem like hours — like when you're waiting to see the dentist — so I thought the journey might seem like forever and back. But what with helping Wallace and the gerbils eat an early lunch and telling stories to Josie, the trip didn't seem as long as I remembered. Soon we turned off the thruway at exit three and began to go along winding roads toward the island. After a bit I saw blue water ahead and we crossed over a bridge, then onto a long causeway. Finally we were on our island.

"I can hardly wait to get cooled off in the ocean," I said.

About a quarter of a mile along the main street we turned down a long, narrow lane. And there at the end of the lane was our white

cottage with blue shutters. And in back of Blue Shutters was the sparkling blue sea.

The car had barely stopped before Wallace and I were out. We took off our shoes and ran down to the rocky beach. The seaweed left from the last tide was already starting to stiffen. It felt half slippery and half prickly to our feet as we made our way into the ocean.

Josie followed right behind and took off all her clothes! Then she sat her bare self down in the cold water. She looked ecstatic. I almost wished I could do that, too.

"Some of these stones are sharp on my feet," moaned Wallace.

"Your feet will soon toughen up," I said as I watched two sea gulls glide up and down on air currents. They were beautiful big birds. I stretched out my arms and exclaimed, "Oh Wallace, isn't it good to be back!"

"Yes," Wallace answered. "And who knows, maybe something exciting will happen." He looked pleased with the idea.

"Once is more than enough, Wallace Crocker!"

I was looking around for unusual seashells to add to my collection when Mom called us to come help unpack. Well, I figured we'd be there all summer to hunt for sea treasures. So

Wallace and I dressed Josie as best we could and went up to help.

By dinnertime we were just about settled in.

"You look happy, Marge," said my father as he worked with Mother in the kitchen. "It's your new business venture, isn't it?" Mother nodded. She was going to open an antique shop at the Algonquin, the big island hotel. Wallace had told his friends that she was going to make pots of money. I wouldn't mind if she did.

"I wish I were going to be here to help you get started," said Dad. He was leaving the next day on a business trip to Japan.

"Oh, I'll be fine with my two helpers," said Mom. She meant Wallace and me. I'm sure she didn't mean Josie.

"She'll be fine if we don't get kidnapped again," Wallace said playfully. His beady little brown eyes twinkled in fun. But my father quickly added, "Now Wallace, don't you worry your mother this summer. She has a right to have her new business go well." We agreed. But we soon found out that not everyone else felt the same way.

2

The Accident

The next morning Mom left Wallace and me to clean up after breakfast while she drove Dad to the airport. Since she took Josie with her, Wallace and I were able to rush through our kitchen jobs and get outside.

It was another hot and dry day. Wallace flopped down with his back against a big pine tree. He had a huge ball of tangled fishing line. It's very frustrating work untangling a fishing line. The dry pine needles crackled as he impatiently shifted his position. "Too dry," he said. "These pine needles—everything—it looks like we need rain."

I started to take my bicycle apart to clean out the dirt and beach sand. "Yeah," I said. "Mom says the fire chief is worried about fires—he posted a notice at the post office. No more beach fires until we've had some rain."

I took a clean rag out of my pocket and started wiping the bicycle spokes. "I guess the other night some campers left their fire going all night. Did you hear Mom tell Dad about it last night?"

"So?" grunted Wallace.

"Well, it caught onto the underbrush. Almost burned the people in the tent. Fires can be a problem. People can get burned up in a house while they sleep."

"I wouldn't," said Wallace. "I'd wake up." Wallace always thinks things won't happen to him, but they do—all the time. To me, too.

"You might not wake up," I said. "That does happen—I hear it on the news sometimes."

"Yeah—well," started Wallace, "some crazy people actually start fires for spite or something." But he didn't finish his sentence because he suddenly sucked in his breath with pain, then he howled at the realization of what he'd done.

That's Wallace, I thought at first. Always makes a big deal out of things. Always thinking he just killed himself or discovered smugglers or got involved in a mystery—overdramatizes, my mother says. But when I looked over and saw the rusty fishhook sticking out of the palm of his hand, I knew he wasn't overdramatizing. Black hook, white skin and the beginning of red blood. It looked awful.

"Oooooh—ow," moaned Wallace, as he tried to remove the fishhook. Then when he found out he couldn't get the thing out, he let out a real howl—and panicked! Blood began to drip as he danced up and down with discomfort.

"Now you know how a fish feels," I said, trying to be calm while I thought of what to do next. The blood bothered me more than Wallace's hopping around. And Mother and the car were gone to the airport.

"We need help," I said. "A doctor, maybe."

"No, no!" yelled Wallace. "He'll hurt."

I've mentioned that Blue Shutters is very secluded, down a long dirt lane. And this is all very nice unless you're in trouble—which we were—and need help. My bike happened to be in pieces, and anyhow a bike was out of the question. With a fishhook in his hand,

Wallace couldn't hold on to me very well. What to do?

"Well, we gotta get some help or you might bleed to death," I said as I pushed him ahead of me up the lane. I figured we'd go on up to Beech Street and see if our friend Dave was in and could help.

As long as the fishhook stayed in, there was nothing we could do to stop the bleeding. And the thought that he might bleed to death kept Wallace moving on the rocky lane, in spite of his bare feet.

When we got up to Beech Street, Dave wasn't home. In fact, nobody was home at his house. And nobody was home at any of the other four houses on the street, either. This wasn't too great a feeling for me. Wallace's loud fear had become a more quiet, desperate kind of fear and his face was white and drawn.

We continued heading down the street and out onto the main road, leaving a dotted trail of blood on the tarred road.

By this time, we were so scared that we practically fell in front of the first car that came along. It didn't occur to us that we might get run over. The little gray car came to a screeching halt about six inches from where we were standing. I recognized the car as belonging to my mother's business friend, Mrs. Emerson, who owned the Algonquin Hotel. But the face that popped out of the window looked anything but friendly. She began to yell something about careless and unattended children but stopped abruptly when she recognized us. And when she noticed Wallace's bleeding hand, she said matter-of-factly, "Well, I see you're in trouble. Get in the car. I'll drop you off at Dr. Jim's office on my way to the hotel."

As we started to get into the backseat, she frowned and said, "You're not to get blood in my car, do you hear?"

I quickly gave Wallace my sweater to hold underneath his hand. That seemed to satisfy Mrs. Emerson. Off we headed for Dr. Jim's office.

Mrs. Emerson is always very businesslike. You couldn't call her a jolly person by any means. I certainly couldn't imagine her offering her lap and a bedtime story to anyone.

We drove without anyone's saying a word— past the island post office and general store, Miss Lacey's antique shop, and the little school.

When we arrived at the doctor's house, we said thank you and got out of the car. As I turned to close the door, Mrs. Emerson said,

"I have a very busy day today, so you're lucky that I was going your way."

I began to wonder if she would have given us a ride if she hadn't been going in that direction anyway.

Dr. Jim must have seen us coming up the path because he was waiting for us at the door. He had a smile on his weather-beaten face and a towel in his hand.

Wallace looked up at Dr. Jim and choked out, "I need a transfusion!"

3

A Threat

Dr. Jim smiled and said, "You can afford to lose a little blood, Wallace, but I can't afford to have it on my new carpet." And he put the towel under Wallace's sweater-wrapped hand and led him into his treatment room. Dr. Jim has a jolly old face and a twinkle in his small blue eyes. He is so old that he even fought in the Second World War. That's where he got his limp, from a gunshot wound.

"A little blood," I thought. It seemed to me as though Wallace had lost six quarts of blood already. But here was a doctor—someone who really knew—actually joking about the whole thing. That made me feel better.

As he helped Wallace up on the table, he said, "You certainly must have impressed Mrs. Emerson, because she isn't programmed to pick up survivors. And just what are you kids going to do this summer? You certainly managed some exciting times last year."

Neither of us answered. Wallace was lying absolutely rigid on the table, trying hard to be brave while Dr. Jim unwrapped his hand. My knees felt wobbly, and my brain was thinking that fixing up Wallace might be something I didn't want to watch.

Dr. Jim looked at the fishhook, "My, my, you really did it. Now Wallace," he said as he picked up a needle, "this is going to hurt a little, but then you won't feel anything. It's an anesthetic." Wallace nodded and mumbled, "OK," but when the needle went in he let out a bloodcurdling howl!

Once I had wanted to be a doctor—as recently as this morning, in fact. But now I really wasn't so interested. Everything in the room began to sort of wave around in my vision.

Doctors must have eyes in the back of their heads. Without taking his eyes from where he was working on Wallace, Dr. Jim said, "Slide down onto the floor, Annie, and put your head between your knees. Then when you feel better go out into the waiting room and admire my new carpet. We don't need you here."

I started to do all of those things when Wallace yelled, "I do. I do need Annie. Besides, Annie is going to be a doctor and nothing bothers her."

I thought a moment. It's nice when someone needs you. Lots of times Wallace has told me to get lost when I didn't want to get lost. Man, I'd love to get that on tape, Wallace actually saying he needed me! I'd play it back to him so many times that the tape would get all worn out. But I wasn't too sure about this kind of needing.

Dr. Jim rescued me. He peered over his half-glasses and said, "Are you really going to be a doctor?"

"A doctor—" I stammered, trying to look anywhere but at Wallace. "Ah—mm—yes. At least this morning I was going to be a doctor."

Dr. Jim stopped a moment to think. Then he said, "Tell you what—why don't you get that high stool over there and sit where you and Wallace can look at each other. You'd be a big help to me by talking to Wallace—and, of course, if you're going to be a doctor, this will give you your first lesson in bedside manner."

So that's what I did! No more wobbly knees and dizzy head. Frankly, I was relieved because I just knew that if I'd gone out to admire the carpet, Wallace would have called me "chicken" the rest of my life.

As he went back to work, Dr. Jim asked us if we'd been out camping yet. I said we planned to go as soon as we could get hold of Dave Stone.

"Well, don't light any fires," he said. "We're all worried with everything so dry. No more beach fires until we've had some rain. I had to treat some campers for burns the other night—nasty business."

Once we started to talk about camping, Wallace began to revive. He told Dr. Jim all about our best camping places, including Gull Island and the small hilly beach behind the hotel called Shannon's Point. His beady little eyes began to shine as they hadn't since his fishhook accident.

"Almost done," muttered Dr. Jim. "Well," he continued, "I dare say that Dave knows more than most folks around here about island life, with his dad being a tugboat captain."

"He says that he has salt water in his veins," I added. Then I giggled. "If he ever needed a transfusion, all you'd have to do is go down to the wharf for a bucket of salt water."

Wallace ignored my humor, but Dr. Jim chuckled.

"Could I go camping as soon as tonight?" asked Wallace.

"Why not?" Dr. Jim answered. "Just as long as you don't get your arm wet." He straightened up from where he had been working. "All finished. Now I'm going to drive you kids home, so let's get going because I have to check on someone who is sick at the hotel."

Wallace said he felt a bit wobbly when he got up. "Yes, well, take it easy for a few hours and you'll be OK," said Dr. Jim.

On the way back around the island, Dr. Jim was quite chatty. "When is your mother going to open up her antique business at the hotel?" he asked.

"Any day now," I answered. "She's just waiting for her shipment of antiques to arrive."

As we drove by Miss Lacey's antique shop, Wallace said, "Well there's one person in the antique business who hopes that my mother's shipment never arrives!"

Dr. Jim laughed. "I'd say that everyone knows about that. Miss Lacey has been hoping for years to open up a shop in the hotel. And now your mother beats her to it."

As we turned into the lane to Blue Shutters, I was relieved to see Mother's car in the parking area. We got out of the car and said thanks to Dr. Jim. "Do try and stay away from rusty fishhooks for a while," Dr. Jim called out after us. Then he drove back toward the hotel.

Well, you should have heard Wallace. What a performance he gave for Mother and Josie with his big bandaged hand! Mother gave him lots of sympathy. She said how lucky we were that Mrs. Emerson happened by. "What next for you two?" she muttered. I'm glad Mother didn't have a crystal ball.

There was such a fuss made over Wallace's hand that I started to get disgusted. I decided to climb up into the big oak tree for some peace and quiet. The heavy leaf growth made the hideaway very secluded; soon the world below was completely blotted out. I couldn't see a thing outside until I got up higher and found an open space where a storm had torn away some branches. The opening was on the water side, giving a wonderful view of our side of the hotel, with Dr. Jim's house nearby.

As I looked over toward the hotel again, I saw Mrs. Emerson's car leave the main parking lot. The car disappeared into the first patch of trees. I waited. Maybe it was going to stop at one of the stores. Nope. It wove in and out of my view and finally vanished for good near Beech Street.

I took another look around the area. I spotted a few people fishing, but nothing else seemed to be going on, so I decided to climb down and join Wallace, who was slumped over under the tree. He had used up all the sympathy he could find and was now a miserable blob.

I had just gotten down from the tree when Mrs. Emerson's car came down the lane. It stopped in front of our house.

Mrs. Emerson hardly noticed us when she got out of her car. Her face looked very strained and serious but she did manage a nod in the direction of Wallace's bandaged hand. Then she went straight into the house to find my mother.

Wallace and I didn't exactly mean to eavesdrop, but the house is so small that with the windows open you can't help hearing what's going on inside.

"I'm so upset," we heard her say.

Mother mumbled something comforting as she put on the kettle and got out some tea mugs.

Mrs. Emerson went on. "I just had to fire Dunbar Harris, my pastry chef at the hotel. It was all so unpleasant. He was caught with hotel silverware, ashtrays, blankets—all kinds of hotel property—in his room."

"Oh?" Mother replied.

"Yes," continued Mrs. Emerson, "and when I confronted him, he got very nasty. Do you know what he threatened to do?"

Wallace and I looked at each other, intrigued.

4

What Happened That Night

Wallace's eyes were sparkling. He has one of those faces that's as easy to read as a book. Big and round and freckled, with no place to hide any secrets. If Wallace feels something, you can always read it on his face. This time his face spelled curiosity.

I was curious, too. But my face doesn't read like a book. You can't always see too much of it, anyhow, with all of my long, brown hair flopping around.

We both inched closer to the house to try to hear better.

"He did what?" we heard my mother ask.

"He threatened to burn the hotel down," said Mrs. Emerson. "And he seemed so, sort of—well—WILD, that I found it most upsetting. And that was after I had agreed not to press charges."

"Well, he probably was so angry at being caught stealing and getting fired that he wanted to get back at you," Mother replied. I know she was trying to be comforting. Still and all, her voice sounded concerned.

I wanted to hear more, so I gently pushed open the screen door and stepped quietly inside the kitchen. Wallace was right behind me. The two women were sitting at the kitchen table drinking tea. I don't think they noticed us standing there.

Mrs. Emerson reached for the sugar and said, "Well, as long as it's just a threat I suppose I can stand it. But I'll be glad when he leaves tomorrow!"

I felt Wallace vibrating next to me. Sometimes he just can't keep his mouth shut. "Dave's father says that the wood in the hotel is so old and dry," he blurted out, "that the sprinkler system might not be much help if a fire really got started—especially when everything is so dry right now—"

"Wallace," I hissed, "why don't you just shut up! Dr. Jim should have anesthetized your voice box while he was at it!"

Mrs. Emerson seemed to get even more distressed by Wallace's remark. Her shoulders sagged. "I'm well aware of that," she said gloomily.

Wallace realized that he hadn't been particularly helpful. He stared down at an antique chest of drawers that my mother was refinishing. I looked down at the chest of drawers too. In fact, almost bored two holes through the top with my eyes.

For what seemed like an endless time no one knew what to say.

The silence was broken by Josie, who came toddling in from the side porch. She didn't realize that anyone was upset. "Annie," she said to me, "I wan' some candy." She hadn't forgotten that we'd promised to take her to the general store.

Wallace and I were relieved for a chance to get out of the gloomy atmosphere, so we both said, "Sure, Josie," at the same time.

But when the three of us got out into the yard Wallace changed his mind. "I don't really feel like going—do you mind?" he asked. He sank down onto the pine needles with his back against the pine tree. The anesthetic had worn off and his hand had begun to throb. I could tell because pain was written all over Wallace's face, as clear as a neon sign.

I reluctantly agreed to take Josie by myself. Wallace rather clumsily held Mom's bicycle while I lifted Josie up into the car seat and tightened the strap. As we started on up the dirt lane I heard Mom yell, "You be careful!" Mothers and dads are like that—always worrying. If she'd been able to see into the next few days she would have been frantic—so I guess it's best she couldn't.

Josie and I were riding along down Beech Street when Dave Stone rode up beside us on his bike. "Glad to see you're back," he said. He's a person of few words and hardly ever gets excited over things the way Wallace and I do.

"I was coming down to see if you wanted to go camping tonight, but what about Wallace and his hand?" he asked.

I was surprised. News travels fast, especially on an island. "Oh, Dr. Jim said that Wallace will be OK by sundown," I said.

"Swell," Dave answered. Swell is only one word, but I knew that it meant everything was all set.

"Me, too," added Josie delightedly.

We laughed. We didn't take a three-year-old very seriously.

We bicycled around past the post office and the little store and had almost gone beyond Miss Lacey's shop when I stopped and turned back. "Hey, Dave," I said, "sleigh bells." I'd always wanted a string of sleigh bells.

Miss Lacey was out in the yard arranging some of her antiques. She's a short, skinny woman with wisps of thin gray hair going in several different directions all over her head. My mother says that Miss Lacey is older than God—and I don't think she means that as a compliment. But then, my mother and Miss Lacey don't have very many nice things to say about each other. For that reason I figured she might not be too friendly.

She wasn't. Looked me up and down coolly. When I asked her about the bells, she snorted and said, "Why don't you get your mother to find you some sleigh bells? She fancies she's in the antique business. And she seems to be able to get anything she wants around here!" Then she turned her back on me and walked off toward the house. As she opened the door I heard her mutter what sounded like, "But she won't have a shop in the hotel if I can help it."

She spoke so softly that only I could hear her. Although I remembered this comment later, I didn't think much about it at the time. At least not enough to tell anyone.

"My dad says she gets meaner every year," said Dave as we started on again to the general store. But soon the whole episode was forgotten as we got involved helping Josie choose her candy. She wanted chocolate bars, peppermint patties, tootsie pops, and red hots—so we had to do some fancy talking to limit her to the money we had. Dave and I bought some jelly donuts and peanut butter crackers for our night out camping.

When we got back home, Mrs. Emerson had gone and Mom was out in the yard sanding the chest of drawers. Wallace was still under the tree reading a book. He was glad to see Dave. "Thought you'd never get here," he said. He looked hot, but at least more alive than when Josie and I had left. Dave and I joined him under the tree and the three of us talked over where we'd camp.

"Have a good time—just don't light any fires right now," Mother called to us. She smiled, and as I looked at her in her faded jeans and red shirt I thought that even if she was 35 years old, she was still kind of pretty.

After much discussion we finally decided to go to Shannon's Point, which is on the other side of the tall pines that encircle the entire hotel property including the hotel's barns and garage. Shannon's Point is very private, and since there is a little hill that might catch any cool breezes, we thought it would be cooler there than any other spot.

Right after dinner we packed our gear in Dave's motorboat and started off toward the point. Wallace wasn't much help because his hand still throbbed—but he was game to go.

When we arrived at the point, we found a good level spot just above the high water mark and rolled out our sleeping bags. For a long time we just sat around eating the jelly donuts and peanut butter crackers and watching it get dark.

Through the pines we could see the lights go on one by one at the hotel. Soon the whole building was lit. Overhead the stars appeared in their nightly patterns, and off in the distance the glow of electric lights started dotting the mainland.

With darkness it began to cool off some. We talked for a while, but eventually we got sleepy and crawled into our sleeping bags. Just before I went to sleep, I looked over at the hotel again—still all lit up. But then, people on vacation like to stay up late.

It seemed like only minutes later that I was startled awake. I don't know whether I woke because of the smell of smoke or the wail of fire engines. Actually, it must have been quite late at night because the electric glow from the mainland was down to a few dots of light here and there. The smell of smoke became stronger by the minute. And when I looked through the trees I saw flames shooting out of the upstairs windows of the barn farthest away from the hotel. It was a very scary sight. The shopping arcade was located in this building and it was where Mom was going to have her new shop. I glanced over quickly at Wallace sleeping soundly and remembered how he'd bragged earlier about waking up if there were a fire.

5
The Missing Dunbar Harris

"Fire! Fire!" I yelled as I kicked the sleeping bags to wake up Wallace and Dave. Through the trees they easily could see the vivid orange flames shooting out of the barn, and could hear the sound of the sirens and smell the smoke. And for the second time in 24 hours, Wallace looked scared. The fear was there on his face as plain as day. Even Dave, who never gets too excited about things, stood there with his mouth open.

"Isn't that burning building the one where the hotel workers sleep?" shouted Wallace.

"Yes," said Dave. "Except for the first floor, because that's where the shopping arcade is. The workers sleep on the next three floors."

When they mentioned hotel workers, I thought of Dunbar Harris, the pastry chef— and his threat to burn down the hotel. I shuddered. "Let's see if the hotel guests need any help."

As we left our sleeping bags and hurried through the stand of evergreens, we could hear more sirens racing toward the fire. The flames leaping from the nearby burning building cast eerie dancing shadows across the hotel lawn. When we opened the lobby door, we found that it was so full of panicky guests that we could hardly get in. Most of them were in their nightclothes. Some of them had suitcases with their belongings. One woman had her fur coat on over her nightgown and a jewel box under her arm. A tall, fat man had his golf bag and clubs slung over his shoulder.

"All the guests must have been warned," muttered Dave.

"Yes," said Wallace, "and it looks like they're scared the fire might spread to this part of the hotel."

"At least they're ready for it," I answered. "More ready, anyway, than the hotel workers were when the barn started to burn. I sure hope that no one was burned up in bed." Even the thought of such a thing sent chilly prickles down my spine.

Wallace's beady little eyes were darting back and forth. "Let's go see!" he said.

The three of us went back out onto the walk, where we found ourselves face to face with fire fighters in black raincoats and hats, and high boots. They were all hurrying around and shouting back and forth. As we turned the corner of the hotel and arrived at the side of the building that faces the barn, we were almost blinded by the bright flames that were rapidly eating away at the old building. The burning timbers gave off an intense heat and each time one crashed down it sent an explosion of sparks into the sky—almost like a Fourth of July fireworks display. The large parking lot between us and the fire was full of fire engines from neighboring towns, and the pavement itself was so covered with fire hoses that I wondered how the fire fighters knew one hose from the other. Police were trying to limit the area to those on official business, but there were still a lot of people milling about—mostly tripping over the tangle of hoses and getting in the way.

By now the whole building was ablaze so the insides of the little shops on the ground floor were completely lit up by the fire. I could see a beach hat and bathing suit display hanging in the window of one of the stores. Then I noticed one empty shop. Seeing it made me sad. "Well, there goes Mother's business venture," I mumbled.

"Yeah, well," said Wallace, "now she'll have to find another place. At least her antiques weren't stored in there."

I noticed that some fire fighters were hosing down the building next to the barn, trying to keep it from catching fire.

"She ought to bury the hatchet and go into business with Miss Lacey," Wallace continued.

"Fat chance," answered Dave. "No one could get along with her. My mother says that Miss Lacey is pretty crazy. Probably even crazy enough to burn down a building!"

Just then I caught sight of Mrs. Emerson talking to the police chief. They looked very serious. I inched over to see if I could eavesdrop on their conversation.

"Yes, yes," I heard her say. "All the people who lived in the barn up over the shops have been found—except Dunbar Harris. No one has seen him."

The police chief said, "And what work did this Dunbar Harris do at the hotel?"

"Well," said Mrs. Emerson, "he was the pastry chef until yesterday."

"And what happened yesterday?" asked the police chief.

"I fired him," Mrs. Emerson answered. Then she proceeded to tell the whole story about why she had fired him and what he had said about burning the hotel down.

"Can you describe Dunbar Harris for me?" asked the police chief.

"Well, he has bright red curly hair, which he wears in a ponytail—and he's short and squarely built," replied Mrs. Emerson.

Wallace and Dave joined me in eavesdropping. "Wow," said Wallace, "this Dunbar Harris sounds weird to me. I bet he burned the place down for spite." Wallace often jumps to conclusions, but I must admit that it looked very suspicious to me, too.

"Well, I don't know," said Dave. "Maybe, just maybe, he didn't burn it down at all. Maybe someone else did and maybe Dunbar got burned up, too."

Wallace and I both thought that this was highly unlikely. It seemed like an open-and-shut case to us. Mrs. Emerson and the police chief continued talking. "Do you know anyone else who might have a grudge against you?" he asked.

"Do you think the fire could have been set?" she asked. "I guess I thought that with the old buildings made of wood and the season being so dry, perhaps someone was careless with a lighted cigarette and it just caught fire."

"Well, we haven't actually found any clues yet," the fire chief added, "but from the way the building went up, it does seem suspicious."

Mrs. Emerson thought a moment longer, then said, "Well, outside of Dunbar Harris, there is one person on the island who has a great dislike for me. And I'll admit she is a bit—well, different. But I'm certain she'd never go around burning buildings."

"Her name?" asked the chief. Then he smiled wryly and said, "Never mind, I already know." On a small island there are never very many secrets.

I could see big pieces of burning debris being swept skyward by a rising wind. It made me worry where they might land on the island. With everything so dry, these flying torches could cause other fires. It was scary. I sure hoped there weren't any problems down at Blue Shutters.

Just then there was a large crash as part of the flaming roof caved in. Police officers were trying to make people move off the hotel property. Over to the left, a team of fire fighters was spraying water over the burning debris as it landed on the other barn. Everything was so dry.

"You youngsters get along home," a tall police officer said to us.

"But we want to help," I said.

"Well, if you want to help," the officer answered, "then go home and tell your parents and neighbors to hose down their roofs and yards. If the wind changes, we may have some problems. We're getting someone to drive all over the island with a loudspeaker to tell people to get out their hoses."

Since there was nothing we could do to help, we started back to Shannon's Point. We headed off into the woods behind the hotel garage. It wasn't a very good path, but it was a shortcut. Fortunately I had my flashlight, so we wouldn't have to trip over any tree roots. As we were weaving in and out of bushes, with me shining my light, the flashlight's beam happened to fall on some cans in the bushes. I would have gone on past them, but there was a strong odor of turpentine coming from them. I'd know the smell anywhere, because my mother uses so much turpentine in her antique business. I stopped and flashed my light down on the cans. The brand name was Big Boy turpentine. It was a different brand from the one my mother uses.

"So, c'mon," said Wallace, "and give us some light, will you?"

"Can't," I answered. "Found something."

The three of us looked down at the cans. I wanted to pick them up and take them back to one of the police officers, but Dave thought that we should leave the cans and get them later. He said it was much more important to get home and start wetting things down.

We continued along without talking, each thinking private thoughts. We were almost back to our campsite when we heard the scraping noise that a boat makes when it's being dragged over pebbles. All three of us stopped. I quickly turned off the flashlight.

"I think someone's at your boat," I whispered to Dave.

"That's silly," said Wallace. "Just who do you think would be out here to steal your boat at this time of night?"

"I don't know who's out there, but Annie is right," answered Dave, "and we'd better find out what's going on."

We moved up as fast as we could. In spite of the light from the fire, this little beach lay in the shadows of tall pines, which made it hard to see much. And we knew it wouldn't be wise to use my light until we got closer. The scraping noise continued until we heard the boat hit the water. My heart was pounding hard, and my hands shook as I quickly turned on my flashlight.

And there, just getting into the boat was a short, squarely built man. His hair was tied in a ponytail, and even in the night light it was plain that his hair was bright red and curly.

For the second time that day, my knees turned to jelly.

6

The Threatening Letter

Wallace seemed frozen to his spot in the beach grass. But Dave quickly knocked the flashlight out of my hands. "If that's who I think it is," he whispered, "he could have a gun!"

Meanwhile, the man in Dave's boat had quickly put the motor in the water and had started her up.

"Bright red curly hair in a ponytail," I whispered. "I bet that's Dunbar Harris. And he's taking your boat!" I began to feel more angry than scared.

"Some nerve," moaned Wallace.

But none of us tried to stop him, because Dave was right—he could have a gun. I thought of the turpentine cans. "Do you suppose that Dunbar is connected to those turpentine cans?" I asked.

"I just bet," said Wallace excitedly. I could practically hear his eyeballs rolling around in his head. "It sure fits together. He must have hid the turpentine cans in the bushes."

"He was just lucky to find my boat," said Dave sadly.

"We are actually helping a criminal escape!" Wallace exclaimed.

I had gotten so mad that I felt like crying. But instead I reached over and felt around for the flashlight in the underbrush. "No time to lose," I said. "We must go tell the police."

We gathered up our belongings and rushed back to the fire. Wallace was so excited that he carried all his camping gear without making one bit of fuss about his hand.

The first police officer we found hardly let us finish our story before he had us back at the campsite. "Time is important," he said. We showed him Dunbar's footprints in the wet sand. Then he checked with Mrs. Emerson and the chief to see if Dunbar had turned up, but he still was reported missing. Finally the officer sent out instructions on his squad car radio to neighboring police to be on the lookout for Dunbar. "At least that's who it seems we should be looking for," he said. "And now I'm going to give you kids a ride home. Why, it's almost daylight!"

Mother was in the yard hosing things down. Although the fire was not flaring up as high as it had earlier, it was still visible from the yard. "I wasn't too worried about you since you were camping," she said, "but I'm glad you're back."

Mom looked sad. I knew it was because her shop had burned.

"I'm sorry about your business, Mom," I said. "Now what will you do when your antique shipment comes?"

"Well," she said, "I'll just have to find another shop to rent somewhere." Then she changed the subject and wanted to know all about our adventures. I decided not to tell her about Dunbar, but Wallace started to say something so I gave him a kick in the shins to shut him up. It did, too, except for a loud "Ow!"

We stayed up a while longer to see if the wind was going to shift. Fortunately it didn't and by the time the sun was up the fire had mostly died down.

"Breakfast, breakfast," came Josie's bright voice from the top of the stairs. She had had a good night's sleep.

"No, not breakfast," groaned Wallace. "Sleep." I could hardly believe my ears when I heard Wallace turning down a meal. But suddenly it hit me, too. "Right," I said. "Sleep." We left Mother and Josie and climbed upstairs to our rooms. My tiny bedroom under the eaves is very cozy and generally smells of pine wood, but this morning it was full of an acrid smoke odor. It didn't bother me long, though. I settled down under my grandmother's soft quilt and was soon dead to the world.

It was almost noon when Wallace and I stumbled back downstairs. We could still smell smoke, but when we looked over at the hotel there wasn't any sign of fire.

Mom was dozing on the living room couch. Dave was outside in the yard pushing Josie on the swing. "Good news," he called. "My boat was found on the mainland an hour ago. Dad took me over and I brought it back."

We were pleased. "What about Dunbar?" I asked. "Did they find him, too?"

"No," said Dave. "But they're still looking. Bet he's gone for good. You never can tell though. My dad says that when someone has a real grudge, sometimes they come back and try again."

I decided not to think about that possibility, so I climbed up into the oak tree to have a better look at the hotel. As I climbed, I could see the gardens in front of the white hotel building through the leaves of the tree. A little higher and I could see the whole property — hotel, garage, and one barn, rather black on one side — and a big, gaping black area where the other barn had been. A bulldozer was moving some of the smoldering debris.

I heard some noises down below and looked to see Wallace and Dave climbing up. Wallace climbed very well in spite of all the bandages on his hand.

Even at this height the branches were thick and strong and there was plenty of room for all three of us.

"Wow," said Dave. "Really good view from here. You guys ought to build a tree house."

"Yeah!" exclaimed Wallace, obviously loving the idea. "Just the thing — a tree house! If we'd been up here in a tree house, we might have discovered the fire from the very first."

Sometimes Wallace gets carried away with his imagination and I have to settle him down. "I hardly think that any of us would have been sitting here in a tree house watching the hotel parking lot at two o'clock in the morning," I said.

All three of us liked the idea of a tree house, though. We had just begun our talk about it when a big truck came down the lane. It was Mother's shipment of antiques!

From our perch in the tree we watched the antiques being uncrated and stored in the empty shed next to Blue Shutters. The men were careful with the antiques, but they left the crates and boards strewn all over the yard.

We climbed down to have a look at things when suddenly a great idea came to me. "These boards would be great to use for a tree house!" I exclaimed.

Wallace and Dave stopped rummaging around and stared at Mother expectantly. Dave seemed normally interested but Wallace looked positively entranced. I feel good that he sometimes likes my ideas, so when he steals one from me I'm almost flattered.

Mother thought a long moment and then she said, "Why not? I won't be needing them."

Wallace surveyed the large pile of lumber and whooped, "It's like Christmas," he yelled.

Even Dave smiled.

The three of us then set to work pulling all the twisted nails out of the wood. It was a hard job, but before long most of the boards were clear, ready to use.

"We need new nails," I said. So we all headed for the island store on our bikes. Wallace was a bit wobbly with his bandaged hand. We parked next to Miss Lacey's little red car with the big daisy painted on the back. As I walked by the car I happened to look inside and see a can of turpentine in the back seat. Since a lot of people use turpentine, I didn't think much about it. But the image did stay in my brain. On our way into the store we bumped into Miss Lacey. She had on a rather dirty plaid dress, and her frizzled hair was off in all directions.

"Too bad your mother's antiques got burned up in the fire," she said. I thought she looked almost happy about it.

"But they weren't," I said.

Miss Lacey looked stunned. "Oh?" she said.

"The antiques didn't come until this afternoon," said Wallace. "And now they're safely stored in our shed until Mom finds a new place for her shop."

Miss Lacey looked very angry. Her face got red and the veins stood out on her neck. She didn't say another word, just turned quickly and left the store. As I watched her drive off in her little red car with the big daisy, I thought of how out of keeping her car was with her personality.

We found that the little store didn't have any nails. We'd have to go into Harborside to do our shopping. But when we got back to Blue Shutters, Mom was almost finished making dinner and said that our trip would have to wait until the next day. She invited Dave to join us for dinner. "Such as it is," she added.

We were in the midst of eating when Mrs. Emerson stopped by. She looked really worried. "Well," she said, "I guess we haven't heard the last from Dunbar Harris—or whoever it was. We received a note saying that yesterday's fire wouldn't be the end. It threatens to burn down the other barn, too."

We all looked at each other. This was a bad turn of events! Before any of us could speak, Mrs. Emerson added, "The strange thing about this note is that it had an island postmark on it. Why on earth he'd want to risk staying on the island when everyone is looking for him is beyond me. Perhaps, just perhaps, it wasn't Dunbar Harris at all—maybe someone right around here is involved." She nodded significantly.

For a split second my brain flashed on an image of a can of turpentine inside a little red car with a big daisy painted on the back. But in an instant it was gone and it didn't return again until much later.

Mrs. Emerson sighed. "It's such a terrible worry. I'll be glad when they catch someone. The insurance company has hired two detectives to stay at the hotel."

Mom tried to be reassuring, but we could see that she was worried, too.

After Mrs. Emerson left, I climbed up into the tree to have another look at the hotel. Nothing unusual that I could see. Parking lot lit up, the hotel rooms twinkling with lights.

At bedtime, while we were brushing our teeth, I said to Wallace, "You know, I've been thinking about the fire and the note and everything."

"So?" said Wallace, with his mouth full of toothpaste.

"Yes," I continued. "I think we should help Mrs. Emerson by keeping a 24-hour watch on the hotel."

"But Annie," said Wallace, "how could we do that with only three of us—and where would we do it?"

"From the tree house," I said, pleased with myself.

Wallace's beady little eyes gleamed. "Yeah," he said, "it's possible—once we get it built. That is, if they haven't tried setting a fire again by then."

"With the detectives there and everything, I somehow think they won't try again right away. I don't know why I think that, but I do."

I finished brushing my teeth and went off to bed, thinking about being on watch all the time and wondering what good it really would do, and how we would make it work. My windows were wide open to let in the summer air. Gradually I became aware of the soft, little, night sounds and the far-off gurgle of the tidal water, and I found it harder and harder to keep my mind on working. Finally, my mind stopped for the night as I drifted off to sleep.

7

A Surprise

The next morning I awoke to the smell of bacon and the sound of the foghorn. From the one, I knew that breakfast was in the making. And from the other, I knew that it must be one of those hard-to-see days on the ocean. I counted two blasts, then two minutes wait, then two more blasts, and so on. The foghorn tells ships where there are rocks that they might otherwise crash into when the fog is thick. The foghorn keeps up this pattern as long as there is any danger to the ships at sea.

I snuggled down under the covers and thought about Dad in faraway Japan. I wondered whether to write and tell him about the hotel fire and threatening note. But suddenly I remembered the nails and the tree house. In no time I was into my jeans and down the stairs. All else was forgotten.

Wallace was getting breakfast. His bandage had blueberry stains on it. He said his hand felt almost like its old self. But the kitchen was not its old self. It looked as though a hurricane had struck! An empty box of blueberry-muffin mix was under a half-opened package of bacon. Perched carelessly on top of three quarter-pound sticks of butter was a carton of eggs. And the usual cooking equipment—measuring cups, mixing bowls, spoons, and other kitchen items—were scattered over the counters. Wallace is a good cook, but as my mother says, his style is somewhat chaotic.

Mother was sitting on the high stool reading the paper. Josie was attacking a bowl of cereal as though she had never seen food before. She was getting most of it into her mouth, but her chin was all milk-wet and sticky.

"Thought you'd never get up," said Wallace, as he carefully drained some rather burned-looking bacon on a paper towel. "We've got a busy day."

"Nails for the tree house," I said as I spread butter and jam on one of Wallace's blueberry muffins. "Harborside. We've got to bike to the hardware store."

Mom stopped reading the paper and said, "Oh?"

I had an awful feeling that we might get stuck sitting with Josie, but we were lucky. After a moment's thought Mom smiled and said, "OK. I want to strip the paint from the old chest that Dave's father gave me yesterday. So Josie will be all right playing around the yard while I work. But do get me a can of Big Boy turpentine, will you?"

Wallace's eyes absolutely flew open and his jaw dropped. I knew what Wallace was thinking because it completely surprised me, too. But my eyes didn't fly open and my mouth was so full of breakfast that if I had let my jaw drop I would have dumped half-chewed food all over the table. All kinds of lights were flashing in my mind as I recalled the cans in the bushes the night of the fire. The thought that our mother might have anything to do with the fire was absolutely too incredible.

IMPOSSIBLE, I said to myself. Using my best police technique, I asked, "How come you want Big Boy turpentine? You don't usually use that kind."

Wallace was sitting as still as a statue, waiting for Mom's answer. I think he was also holding his breath because his face started to get red.

"In Harborside, they don't sell the kind I'm used to," Mother answered. "Mrs. Emerson says that Big Boy is the only brand sold here, so everyone on the island has to use it."

Wallace let out his breath with a sigh of relief. Then he whooped and danced like crazy around the kitchen. He even kissed Josie on top of her head. Josie didn't think his behavior was unusual, but Mom looked puzzled.

I just knew that Mom couldn't possibly be involved in burning anything down. Especially a place where she was going to have her own shop. But I realized it did pose another problem. Mrs. Emerson had said everyone who painted had to use Big Boy turpentine. So unless there was an open and shut case against Dunbar Harris, this fact could make things more difficult.

My thoughts were interrupted by Mother. "I'll clean up the kitchen so you two can get an early start. Wallace, can you manage a bike with that hand?"

"No problem," said Wallace. "It's almost not sore at all—and there's lots of padding."

We both thanked Mom for taking on the kitchen. Boy, what a mess she had to deal with! As we headed up the lane on our bikes, she called after us, "Be careful of the traffic, won't you?"

Dave was out in his yard kicking a soccer ball around the front lawn. When he saw us, he got on his bike with a curt, "Hi ya." As I've said before, Dave is a person of few words. And he takes time to think things over. He didn't say much even when we told him about our plan for a 24-hour watch in the tree house.

Soon we were out on the causeway. Fog softened the outlines of the small islands on our left. I could just make out, farther off in the distance on a raised part of land, the shape of the Algonquin Hotel emerging like a beautiful white ship through the swirling mist.

At the end of the causeway we took the main road into town. There was so much traffic, with summer tourists driving through town to points north, that Dave said he knew of a better route when we were ready to head back home.

We finally got to the hardware store. The man who waited on us was very friendly. We got the nails and rope—for a ladder—but he had to go down into the cellar to open up a new shipment of Big Boy turpentine. He said that a customer had bought quite a lot of turpentine several days ago.

"Now that I think about it, it was someone out on the island," he said. "Forgot his name."

At that moment I'm certain that the three of us had the same thought—

"Can't you remember it?" asked Wallace, trying his best to sound casual—but actually sounding very eager!

The man stood scratching his head for a few seconds, but finally shrugged his shoulders and shook his head.

We started to leave when I had an idea. "Do you remember what the man looked like?"

"What she means is," added Wallace, "did the man have bright red hair or anything like that?"

The salesman laughed. "My goodness no, not red hair. Red hair is not something you see around here very often. No sir, I'd remember red hair. Besides, a man that age wouldn't have anything but gray hair. Tell you the truth, I don't rightly remember much about him—kind of ordinary-looking, I guess."

Dead end. No luck here. We said thank you and were halfway out the door when we heard the salesman say, "Come to think of it, I did notice one thing—he had a limp. I remembered it just now because I saw it as he went out the door."

I mumbled, "Thanks," and we left to go back home.

"Not much help, was he?" said Dave as we unlocked our bikes.

Wallace was standing still holding his bike lock, staring off into space. "Gray hair—a limp—that means just one person I know of on the island. Dr. Jim!"

"Dr. Jim!" yelled Dave. "You're crazy, how could Dr. Jim—"

"He lives next to the hotel," said Wallace. "And besides, I didn't say he did anything, did I? And let's get going back or we'll never get anything done today."

For a little while, as we threaded our way through the busy streets, there wasn't much chance to talk. Gradually the traffic began to thin out as Dave took us on side streets. Soon we were well away from the center of town and out onto a wooded road with no houses in sight—just pine trees on either side of the road. At least I didn't notice any houses until we needed some help.

As it happened, we were riding along, minding our own business, when a car came speeding close to the edge of the road. I was last in line, so I saw the whole thing. It passed Dave and me, but almost crowded into Wallace. Wallace swerved to be clear of the car and as he did, his front tire got stuck in a rut and he was thrown off his bike and into a narrow ditch by the roadside.

As I watched the little red car speed off, I saw a big daisy on the back.

"Hey," I yelled, "that was that crazy Miss Lacey! Looked like she wanted to ram into you."

"Maybe she did," said Dave. "She hates your mother enough to hurt you kids."

But this comment was temporarily forgotten as we stopped our bikes and waited for Wallace to get up. He didn't. Or he couldn't. He tried to, but every time he put any weight on his left foot he groaned and fell back.

Dave and I wheeled our bikes into the grass and went over to Wallace. I could see his ankle was beginning to swell. "Oh, Wallace," I

wailed, "not another accident. I can't believe it."

Dave looked down at Wallace's leg. "Maybe it's broken," he said slowly.

That sounded too awful but I knew we needed help because Wallace just couldn't get up. It was then that I saw the little house way back from the road, almost screened by the woods. "C'mon, Dave. Let's see if the people in that house can help us." I thought of asking Dave to stay with Wallace but then decided I wanted Dave to go with me just in case the people had a big dog or something.

There wasn't any dog. But we got the biggest shock of the afternoon when we knocked and the door opened—because there stood a squarely built man of about medium height, with bright red hair tied back in a ponytail. I know Dave was thinking the same thing I was—Dunbar Harris!

My heart began to pound hard, my mouth got dry, and I wanted to turn around and run, but my legs wouldn't obey orders.

8

A New Turn Of Events

I was really scared, I can tell you. And for a second or two, I expected Dunbar to force us into the house and tie us up. But gradually I got enough control of myself to realize that he was just standing there looking at us—with a pleasant smile on his face. "Can I help you?" he asked.

Dave found his tongue first, "Well, 'ah, you see—" As I've said, Dave isn't one to talk your ear off, and when he's scared I guess his words are even slower coming out.

I wanted to say, "No, thanks," and turn around and run. But we did need help, and something about Dunbar's manner made me feel like trusting him. So I told him about Wallace's leg, and in no time Dunbar had gone down and helped Wallace up onto the porch and into a hammock.

Wallace was astounded when he saw Dunbar. But his ankle hurt too much for him to think about anything else.

At first we were all busy helping Dunbar put ice packs on Wallace's ankle. Then as the ice began numbing the ankle, I could see Wallace's beady little eyes start dancing around. He said, "Nice place you've got here," trying to be real cool.

"Yes," said Dunbar. "It isn't mine, though. Belongs to my aunt, but she's away and said I could use it—" he stopped and thought— "while I'm in between jobs, so to speak." Then he changed the subject and said he'd take us home. But when we told him we lived out on the island, he hesitated. He rubbed his chin and said, "I don't know as I'm very popular out there these days."

"Oh," said Wallace innocently. "Why is that?" Wallace is so much better at that fake stuff than I am. As for Dave, he doesn't even know how to do it at all.

Dunbar hesitated. I don't know why he told us, but he did. Maybe he was just lonely. Even crooks get lonely, I guess. So he said slowly, "Well, they fired me at the Algonquin and I got mad and told Mrs. Emerson that I might burn the hotel down. Then darned if part of it didn't burn down that very night!" He almost seemed relieved to be telling us.

I was amazed. In my mind's eye I kept seeing Dunbar pushing off in Dave's boat. I heard myself saying, "You mean you didn't set that fire?"

Then it was Dunbar's turn to be surprised. "You sound as though you thought I did. How come? What do you know about it?" He seemed a little on edge, so I found myself blurting out the whole thing about the cans of turpentine, his stealing Dave's boat, the letter— everything!

Dunbar looked more surprised by the minute. When I finished, he was silent for a few moments. Then he said slowly, "Well, it's true, I did steal a few things. But I am not a firebug. I left the boat where someone would find it. And I certainly did not write that letter. You said it had an island postmark and I haven't been out on the island since the night of the fire. So I couldn't have written it."

Wallace and Dave just sat there, sort of numb with surprise. Ever since the fire, they had felt that Dunbar was guilty, and it was hard for them to change their minds. I believed Dunbar, though. I guess one of the reasons that I believed him was that he was so open about having stolen from the hotel. If I had stolen something, I certainly wouldn't go around admitting it, but then stealing isn't something I'd do anyhow.

"Tell you what," said Dunbar. "I'll take Wallace and his bike as far as the end of the causeway and leave him there by the side of the road. Then you and Dave can cycle on to Blue Shutters and get your mom to pick him up."

Just before we all took off from Dunbar's place, he said, rather firmly, "Now look, I've done you kids a favor. So you do one for me and don't tell anybody you've seen me. Agreed?"

We all nodded.

"And what's more," he continued, "I'll write a note to the chief of police to tell him that I had nothing to do with the fire or the threatening letter. I'm going to Boston tomorrow to look for a job, so I'll send the letter from there."

We said good-bye and thanks and started off on our bikes. Dunbar said he'd give us enough time to get to the causeway before he started out with Wallace. "Watch out for that red car with the daisy," Wallace yelled as Dave and I headed down the drive.

"Did you really mean it when you said Miss Lacey hates Mother enough to hurt us?" I asked Dave as we rode along.

"Yes, I did," said Dave. "My father says she's done some mean things in her day."

"Well, is she nuts enough to burn a building down?"

"Oh, who knows," said Dave. "At least we're pretty certain that Dunbar didn't set the building on fire so now we have to find another suspect." Just at that point we were passing the Ice Cream House but we couldn't stop because Wallace might be waiting at the causeway.

Actually, he was already sitting there in the grass by the time we arrived. Dunbar had not passed us in his car, so I knew they had come by the shortcut.

Right after we arrived at the causeway, Dr. Jim happened to ride by. He saw us and stopped, so we didn't have to go get Mom. As we helped Wallace into the car, Dr. Jim shook his head and said, "Wallace Crocker, I declare, you seem to have a knack for doing mischief to yourself."

Wallace looked miserable again. As a matter of fact, he was so wrapped up in himself that he didn't notice Dr. Jim's limp when he got out of the car. But I noticed it and it set my mind buzzing with what we heard at the hardware store.

When Dave and I got back to Blue Shutters, Dr. Jim was fixing Wallace's ankle. "Just a bad twist," he said.

"So how did it happen?" Mom asked.

We didn't exactly lie, but from the way we answered I think she thought that Wallace had hurt himself on the causeway. We decided it best to let her and Dr. Jim think that—at least for the time being.

"Well," said Dr. Jim as he looked down at Wallace, "a blueberry-stained bandage on your hand, a clean white one on your ankle. Wallace, you are a sight! You can begin to move around when it stops hurting so much. But with your luck, Wallace, I think you might be wise to spend the summer on that couch!" As Dr. Jim limped out of the room, Wallace was obviously more alert because his eyes suddenly rolled around and his jaw dropped.

Dave was the first to say something when Mom left the room with Dr. Jim. "I still can't imagine Dr. Jim lighting any fires. I've known him all my life, and he just isn't the type. Also, he doesn't have a motive. He's the hotel doctor and gets on just fine with Mrs. Emerson."

"So who does have a motive?" asked Wallace. Then he smiled and said, "I know, don't tell me—a little red car with a daisy painted on the back."

"Well, she did force you off the road," said Dave. Then he added, "But she certainly isn't a man with a limp!"

Wallace giggled because Dave didn't make jokes very often.

"She certainly doesn't want Mom to have her antique shop at the hotel," I said, and I told them what Miss Lacey had said the day I'd seen the sleigh bells.

They were very interested. I also told them about seeing the Big Boy turpentine in her car.

Wallace was just about to say something when Mom came back with good news. Mrs. Emerson had stopped by to tell her that she was going to fix up the other barn for the shops again. Now Mom could have her antique shop after all! She looked pleased.

She invited Dave to stay for dinner and even said we could have pizza. "That is, if you'll ride over to the store and get the pizzas," she added. It's amazing how expansive parents can be when they're in a good mood.

I was happy for her, and I wanted her shop to work out this time.

Obviously Wallace couldn't go with us to get the pizzas, so Dave and I set off. As we peddled along I said, "We've got to get the tree house built before the other barn is ready for people to move their shops in."

"The trouble is," said Dave, "we don't know whether we're looking for a 'he' or a 'she' now that Dunbar is cleared."

"Or a 'they,'" I added, as we parked our bikes and went into the pizza parlor.

On our way out, we saw Miss Lacey's red car with the daisy parked next door at the post office. But Miss Lacey wasn't there. Instead, an older man threw a pile of mail into the back seat and then walked around to get into the driver's side. He didn't walk fast because of his limp. I couldn't believe it! "I thought you said Miss Lacey lives alone," I whispered to Dave.

"Well, she does," he answered. "She does, except for when her brother comes—and that's who just got into her car. Must be here for a visit."

Flash in my brain. "But he has a limp."

"Yeah, I know," said Dave. "I guess I forgot about him because he isn't here very often."

"So," I said eagerly, "maybe that lets Dr. Jim off the hook. Miss Lacey's brother could have bought the turpentine."

"Maybe," said Dave. "But how can we prove it?"

When we got home, Mom, still in her jovial mood, was so busy serving us pizza and chattering away that it was almost bedtime before we could get Wallace alone long enough to tell him our latest news. He was very excited. "So I bet that the two of them are in it together— Miss Lacey and her brother. We'd better get that tree house built," he said. "Something is going to happen soon. I can feel it in my bones."

I shivered. It seemed like forever before I could get to sleep that night.

9

The Tree House

The next morning, much to my surprise, Dave was sitting in the kitchen with Mom and Josie when I came downstairs. Wallace limped down in back of me. His ankle was still sore, but was getting better fast.

"Thought you were going to sleep all day," said Dave.

"So let's get busy on the tree house," Wallace answered as he wolfed down a big bowl of cereal.

Well, we did get busy. Or at least Dave and I got busy. Wallace still couldn't do much, so

it didn't go as fast with two people. We hauled
the boards up into the tree by means of a rope.
It was hard work.

"Little faster there," Wallace would shout.
And if a board happened to slip off the rope
and fall to the ground, Wallace would yell,
"What's the matter—you clumsy or something? Anyone could tie that on right!"

He certainly was a tyrant, I can tell you. At
noon Wallace hobbled into the kitchen and made
us some sandwiches so that we could keep working. My arms ached from all the hauling and
hammering. All I can say is that if Dave's father
hadn't stopped by and pitched in to help us, I
don't know when we would have gotten it done.
By late afternoon the tree house was finished
enough to use for a comfortable lookout.

"So," said Wallace eagerly, "we'd better
start our watch right now."

I was beginning to have doubts about the
tree house business, but perhaps it was because
I was so tired.

Wallace may have been in some pain, but he
wasn't as tired as Dave and I, so he was more
optimistic. "Listen, Annie," he said, "I have a
hunch that if the firebug strikes again it will be
at night—like last time—when the shops are
empty and most people are in bed."

"But the hotel has two detectives and a night watchman," said Dave slowly. He sounded a bit doubtful.

"Yes," Wallace answered, "but they can't be everyplace at the same time. We just might spot a fire quicker from here than if we were at ground level at the hotel."

And much to our surprise Wallace volunteered to do his share of the watching. He can be brave at times, I must say, because he climbed up into the tree! It probably hurt his ankle like anything, but he did it. When Mother saw him, she had a fit, but she finally agreed to let him stay.

I handed binoculars up to Wallace, then Dave and I got cushions and some other things to make the tree house comfortable. It didn't take very long and soon the three of us were settled.

"The only thing of any interest I've seen while you have been busy is Miss Lacey's car driving up behind the hotel," said Wallace. "I could tell by the daisy. Her car stayed only a few minutes, but why would she want to drive up behind the hotel?"

Dave started to say something, but stopped when Mrs. Emerson drove up in front of the house. Mother came out to meet her.

Mrs. Emerson looked grim. "The plot thickens, Jane," she said. "We're now pretty certain that it wasn't Dunbar Harris at all."

Mother sounded surprised. I couldn't see either one of them because of the thick covering of leaves and branches. The tree house was so well hidden that no one would even know we were there. I'm certain that Mrs. Emerson thought that Mom was the only person around.

"Yes," continued Mrs. Emerson. "The chief of police received a letter from Dunbar from Boston, telling us that he had nothing to do with the fire. The police and detectives think he's telling the truth. So that leaves us to find out who we're trying to catch, who's doing all this mischief." Then she added in a tone I could just barely hear, "Frankly, I have my suspicions. But accusing someone without evidence isn't any help."

"At any rate," continued Mrs. Emerson, "I just stopped by to tell you that the carpenters are making great progress on the new shops. It won't be long now before your shop will be ready for you to move in. It's lucky your antiques are stored so handily here in your shed."

Mother nodded in agreement and stood for a few minutes, lost in thought as Mrs. Emerson drove out the driveway.

Up in the tree house the three of us were busy thinking.

Finally Dave said, "Well, Dunbar kept his promise about sending the letter."

"Yeah," said Wallace. "So that really lets him off the hook. Boy, I'll just bet that Miss Lacey burned down that barn."

"Well, she's sure mad enough at Mrs. Emerson for letting Mom have her antique shop in the hotel," I said.

"Agreed," said Wallace. "Miss Lacey would give almost anything to have a shop there."

"Of course, she's got her own antique business at her house," said Dave.

"True," I answered, "but she would get a lot more business at a place like the hotel. Money! Mom says people will do a lot of unusual things for money."

Wallace had been lost in thought. Finally he said, "Well, let's look at it this way—if you were a firebug, what part of the hotel would you try burning next time?"

"It depends," I said, "on whether the firebug is Miss Lacey."

"How do you mean?" asked Wallace.

"Well, if it is Miss Lacey, then I expect she'd try and burn down the shops again. But if it's someone who just hates Mrs. Emerson, then

I'd say they might try the main part of the hotel this time."

You won't believe this, but just as I finished saying this, we heard the fire engines scream out of the firehouse. We all scrambled for the binoculars. Wallace got them first. "Can't be the hotel," he said. "All is in order over there as far as I can see—no flames or excitement."

We watched the fire engines race along the road and into the hotel parking lot. The fire fighters jumped off the trucks and started dragging hoses into the remaining barn. Volunteer fire fighters came screeching up in their cars and trucks. They leaped out of their vehicles almost before the engines stopped running. The cars and trucks were left helter-skelter all over the grass.

"Strange," said Wallace. "I still can't see any flames. Blast! I would have to be laid up with this ankle, or I'd go over there."

Since Dave and I didn't have bad ankles, we practically slid down the tree and onto our bikes.

As we started up the lane, I yelled back, "If Mom wants to know where we are, tell her we'll be back soon."

Wallace moaned with frustration.

In no time Dave and I arrived at the hotel. We parked our bikes next to some tall pines. Then we threaded our way over the maze of fire hoses and around little groups of excited people to the back door of the hotel barn. We didn't smell any smoke or hear the crackle of flames. Just as we started to go through the doorway we were stopped by one of the detectives that the insurance company had hired. "Sorry, kids, you'll have to clear out—no one allowed beyond this point."

The detective was pleasant, but he didn't seem particularly chatty. And he looked strong enough to enforce any rules he might have.

I decided to see what I could find out. "Is the fire serious?" I asked politely.

He had a hard set to his jaw. "All fires are serious," he replied.

No information from that. "Try again, Annie," I said to myself. Dave was in one of his more silent moods, so he was no help. I missed Wallace. "We're the kids who found the cans of turpentine in the bushes after the first fire," I continued.

His face lit up. "Oh, yes, the police told us about you." Since he seemed more friendly I decided to try again. And it worked! This time he told us what we wanted to know. And then

Dave and I hurried back to tell Wallace. We were two mighty puzzled people, I can tell you. "Wait until Wallace hears this," I called to Dave as we peddled furiously toward home.

"Yeah," said Dave, "wait until he hears." That's all Dave said the whole time we were gone. Man, he sure can be quiet at times.

Wallace was very glad to see us. We hardly had time to climb back into the tree before he started to throw questions at us.

"Well, Wallace," I said, "you won't believe this, but there really was a second fire. It was in the barn where the new shops are going to be. Not in the hotel. And it was set with lighter fluid on wood shavings in a closet in—guess where?" I waited, teasing Wallace a little.

Wallace was beside himself. "C'mon, Annie," he said. "Tell me the rest!"

"Well, it was in the closet in Mother's antique shop!"

Wallace was astounded. "In Mother's shop! Do you suppose her shop was picked out especially?"

"I wondered the same thing," I said.

"Very suspicious," mumbled Dave. Then he remembered something I'd forgotten to tell Wallace. "There is no sprinkler system in the closet, so the fire had a better chance of catching on."

"Oh, my gosh," said Wallace. "Now where do we go from here?"

"And where will the firebug strike next?" I asked.

"More important," said Wallace, "*who* is the firebug?"

10

A Very Dangerous Evening

It was close to dinnertime when Mom called to us, "Are you going to join Josie and me for dinner? Or would you like a picnic in your tree house?"

"You can serve us up here," Wallace called back. Man, with his two injuries, he was getting very used to being waited on.

"Well I've got news for you, sweetheart," Mom answered. "This mother does not do room service. If you want to eat up there, fine. But you'll have to send one of your slaves down to get your dinner."

I giggled. Mom certainly had Wallace's number.

"Annie, you and Dave fix our dinner," Wallace suggested. "I'll man the binoculars."

It seemed fair, in light of Wallace's bad ankle. So Dave and I climbed down and went into the kitchen to make a picnic for the three of us. Josie wanted to join us, too, but Mom came to our rescue. "No, Josie," she said, "I need you down here to help me make some cookies—peanut butter."

Her favorite kind! Josie beamed and went and got an apron.

It didn't take Dave and me long to put an awful lot of food into a basket and two big shopping bags. We started out with potato chips, dill pickles, tuna sandwiches, and half of a watermelon. When Mom saw us lugging all that food out the door, she made some comment about how it looked as though we were getting ready for a national disaster! Wallace hauled the basket up with a rope and after he emptied it, he sent it down again for us to fill up with the stuff in the bags.

Finally the three of us were settled with our feast. It was a lot of food, but we took our time eating. We kept looking over at the hotel and going over all of the clues we had so far.

"Watching for something to happen is very boring until it actually happens—then it can be exciting," I said.

"And sometimes dangerous," Wallace added hopefully. He wanted some action.

"That's why it's good to eat," said Dave, as he reached for his millionth handful of potato chips. "Helps you pass the time." It's obvious that Dave loves to eat.

"Now, let's see," I said. "Who on the island, besides Miss Lacey, do we know who uses turpentine and hates Mrs. Emerson?"

Dave thought for a minute, then said, "Well, I'm not certain about the turpentine part, but I honestly don't know of anyone else who really hates Mrs. Emerson."

"I still think that Miss Lacey is involved with these fires," I said.

"Remember," said Dave, "this fire was different—there was no turpentine."

"True," I answered. "Do you think there could be more than one firebug?"

Wallace said, "You know, the things we've found out about Miss Lacey really makes her suspect number one—what Annie heard her say, the time she pushed me off the road, which I don't think was an accident, and her brother with the limp. . .." His voice trailed off.

Dave still wasn't fully convinced. "I'll admit it does sound bad for Miss Lacey, but what do we do now?"

"Tail her," I quickly responded.

Wallace and Dave groaned. "Gosh, Annie," said Dave. "How are we going to do a thing like that? We've only got bicycles, and she's got a car."

We were still arguing about what our next move would be when Mom came out to tell us it was bedtime and if we wanted to spend the night up in the tree house, we should come down and get sleeping bags.

So Dave and I climbed down again to get our gear. Dave called his parents who, luckily, said he could stay.

It was getting dark when we finally were all settled in the tree house. The little night noises had begun and a cool breeze was gently moving the leaves. Fireflies flittered here and there. Over in the distance the Algonquin Hotel was cleared of fire trucks, and people were once more going about their vacation pleasures.

We decided to divide the night up into hour-long watches. "But I bet nothing more will happen tonight," I said. How wrong I was.

By 2 o'clock in the morning, we'd each had at least one watch and so far nothing unusual had happened. It was my turn, and I was just taking another look at the hotel when my binoculars happened to catch a car driving past the post office and heading in our direction. I couldn't see what color the car was. I was wondering who would be on the road at that hour of the night when I heard the engine up at the head of the lane. Then it switched off. Silence— for a while. That is, except for the night sounds. I don't know why, but I began to have a funny feeling in the pit of my stomach and prickles on my skin. I woke Dave and Wallace and told them what I'd heard and cautioned them to whisper.

Suddenly our whispers were interrupted by a noise halfway down the lane. It sounded as though someone had stumbled and dropped something heavy—a can, maybe, because of the clanging sound.

"I think someone is coming down here," whispered Wallace.

My mouth got dry. I wondered if that happened to Dave and Wallace, too.

We waited. No sound for a few minutes. The moon was shining, but not much more than tiny patches of moonlight got through where we were.

More waiting—for what seemed like hours. Finally, we heard the soft crunch of footsteps on the gravel. Getting closer to the tree. Wallace and I didn't know it, but we were holding hands. I finally realized it when Wallace's ring began to dig into my finger.

Now the steps sounded close to the tree— but I couldn't see the figure, except for one brief view of the edge of a skirt. It must be a woman. After the person passed through the yard, we heard her steps grow softer as they reached the grass.

Wallace found his voice first. "Got to do something. I'll bet she's going to set fire to our house—and I know who it is. Let's yell and scare her off."

I started to agree, but Dave said, "No, my dad says you've got to actually see someone *do* the thing—"

"What? See her burn the house?" said Wallace. "Now you're crazy!"

"No, we'll just follow her and flash our light when we think she's about to do it. Annie and I will follow her now. You creep inside and get your mother—sore ankle or not."

So that's what we did. Climbed quickly and quietly down from the tree to our various jobs. Although my knees were quite rubbery from fear, I managed to get fairly close to the person. We followed her around the back of our house, but she didn't stop there. She went over to the shed where Mother's antiques were stored. There was the sound of cans being set down, tops unscrewed and the sound and smell of turpentine being poured on the very dry pine needles around the shed. I shuddered. It was so dry that if she did light a match everything would go up very quickly!

Mother and Wallace had just joined us when Dave whispered fiercely, "Now, Annie! Shine your light before she lights that match!" I did.

For a moment we were all horribly stunned, because it wasn't the person we had expected— Miss Lacey. It was Mrs. Emerson, my mother's friend and business associate! Mother walked forward in a daze. "Grace," she began, "what on earth can you be thinking of?"

Mrs. Emerson looked trapped, like a rat. Instead of running, she just stood there in her summer dress looking angrier and angrier and angrier, as if she were going to explode. Finally she started to scream, "You nosey, meddlesome brats. I hate kids. I should never have picked you up the first day." She continued to scream—all kinds of things—most of them incoherent.

Soon we heard the police car, which Mother had called just before she left the house.

Mrs. Emerson's screams were frightening, but they were also kind of sad. She was still yelling when the police took her off in their squad car.

After hosing down the pine needles around the shed, we all went inside with Mom for some hot cocoa and toast, but we kids did all the eating and drinking. Mother was still in shock. She kept muttering, "But why—"

Gradually we got sleepy. Wallace and I went upstairs to bed and Dave went out to sleep on the porch.

That morning, early, the police chief came down to tell us that Mrs. Emerson had confessed to both fires.

"But why did she do it?" we all asked at the same time.

"Well," said the police chief as he settled into a kitchen chair, "it seems that she isn't quite the efficient business person we've thought she is. The Algonquin Hotel was in bad need of major repairs when she bought it. And she had to take out a second mortgage even to buy it. She didn't have any money saved and she owed everyone." He put some sugar in the coffee that Mother had just given him.

Mother was finally perking up a little. "So she burned the building down to get insurance money? But it's so hard to believe—you think you know a person."

"I still don't understand why she tried to burn Mother's antique shed," I said.

"Well, Dunbar gave her the idea in the first place. But then with Dunbar out of the running and with those detectives hanging around, she thought that if she burned your shed and left a scarf belonging to Miss Lacey at the scene it would throw all suspicion on Miss Lacey. Mrs. Emerson was the one who sent that letter, too."

"Golly," said Wallace. "She's crazier than Miss Lacey."

"Well, she's different, anyway," continued the chief. "I'll admit that we could've suspected Miss Lacey, because she is unusual—but her type almost never goes around burning buildings. They're mostly talk."

"Will Mrs. Emerson go to jail?" all three of us asked at once.

"'Fraid so," the chief answered. Then he looked at us with great admiration. "You kids are really something—and we're grateful to you, I must say."

In a way, we felt sorry for Mrs. Emerson, but she had caused so much trouble that we were also relieved.

Word got around the island about our part in solving the mystery, and we were congratulated by everyone we met. It was a nice feeling, knowing that the rest of the summer would be less worrisome for everyone. Dr. Jim was appointed to run the hotel and once he got things going again, we hoped that Mother could still have her shop.

So you see, if it hadn't been for the tree house, we might have been burned up. Which is really pretty awful to think about.

I went outside and looked up through the branches at our tree house. Then I patted the tree trunk and said softly, "Thanks, you good old tree."